Withered Shoe Strings

Forest York

Text Copyright © Forest D. York, 2020
Austin, Tx
All Rights Reserved

Paperback ISBN 978-0-9896438-4-9
Ebook ISBN 978-0-9896438-5-6

I suppose that even the world itself could not contain the books that should be written. Amen.

John 21:25b (KJV)

For Sonia, for always

Table of Contents

LIFE

Poster Child
On Dirt
Odyssey
Wolf Hospital
Ending (part 1)
Glimmering History
Cake Plaster
morNING
Breakened
Wintum
Rosy Red Cheeks
Litotes
Chilled Lips
Blotches
ANT HILL
Let us
Grassroots
Sweats
Dirty Mind
Mineful
Under-Bite your tongue
Summer
Still, be.
Good Morning, Moon
Mind of the Life
Automatic for the people
Strawberry Steamboat
Nobody Travels Anymore
Hollywood

Woodn't *
Steeped in the Sway of Surrender
EID
Sunny Side Up
Αρχική
Cages
Inside the mind of a shivering swan, withering fawn
Deciduous
giAnTS
Over-Bite my tongue
Is Bliss
Radiator's Smoking
Fingers
A Call
Crunched Tooth
New Born Dotage
Salesmen
Splitting Headache
Thursday
                DEATH
Aged Friends
Adorable
Ending (part 2)
Bechildrened Head
Buster Speedometer
Daily Coffins
Oranges
Chest Garden
Make-Up
Isabella
Weirdo
/A\
Thunders of Many

Plywood Walls
America, the Beautiful
Crosby
Young
Skid Marks
Craters of plaster and paper and pasture
Dark Night
Civil War
Pen to Pad
Rain Check
Alls Timer
The Coast
Favoritistic
Saudade
Gymnastics
Splintered
trash
Soggy Drawers
Mau Ofs
Chubby Bunny
P-acrimonious Man
The Ascension
Wet Jeans
REBIRTH
Flame Retardant
Ten Thousand Years
be
Ending (part 3)
Blood Hiccups
Selfie
The Hills Have Eyes
FI EL DS
CUP

Pimples
Nature's A Dictionary
Raven Wings/Wedding Feast

Glasses
At The End Of The Day *
Supplication
Facelessly
Forfeit
Brittle STRucturrrre e s...
Recycling
Botched Carpentry
powerless saviours
Eight of Them, Already
.Smokeless Campfire.
Birthing classes
Lady MacBeth
the darkest alley
Understandable for some, but not for me. I don't
        understand it. I want to though... (The Title)
Bastion
Resplendent Birth
Hiraeth
A Frame
Yearbooks
Townie

Poster Child

When I dug out the root from underneath the tree,
I thought I caught a glimpse of the other side
But its resemblance too quickly dissolved in the ground
And the fascination with worlds unknown died.

When I die bury me in the roots underneath the tree
for I will have passed from the world and died
But as my resemblance too quickly dissolves in the ground,
I will find Your prints on the other side.

LIFE

On Dirt

On such a brightened day as this,
the wind betrays my flimsy shirt.
It swiftens close for me a kiss,
of caustic and telluric dirt

Odyssey

    As my eyes closed, the words began to slow and spread further and further apart.
Space is where I live, searching the heavens for air, bumping into stars. Ability is what keeps me wondering where you are. The earth, a distant sphere, unfamiliar and foreign, like a memory of some place I've never been, created only by rumors and hearsay.
I miss most the taste of pasta: isn't that sad? The cravings of a man on death row, as if the last meal is worth it: black beans slow cooked with a dab of red wine vinegar and garlic, steak, potatoes mashed with a fork and a touch of paprika, the list goes on. My last meal, I couldn't care less the food served, but let me eat with my wife, my family, and my friends. Anyone. Is the fear of being alone valid? You have made so many of us, yet we're blinded to each other. I wonder, to what other needs have we blinded ourselves? Have we needed something we disregarded as inane?
I don't know...
I don't know.

Space is so far, obviously we haven't miss anything yet.

Wolf Hospital

Cigars and rhubarb taken during the raid;
A little girl's screaming only takes a few yards to fade
as they sneak and get away.

Ending

Part 1)
He doesn't mind thinking about life with no death, it doesn't seem to affect the day to day.
If he did die, and done is done, would he have been like a baby before being born.
Do the unborn now sit like a puzzle of possibilities in some peaceful place?
Where is each mind before life?
Christ was alive before his birth, but His birth brought Himself to us and us to Him.
Death seems to be the easy part. Living is difficult.

Glimmering History

The damp from the morning's dew soaked through his socks and the back of his jeans as the screen door was slammed behind him, bouncing until it tired out. His friend had a green thumb and he wanted to show her that he could grow plants, flowers, and vegetables in his garden as well. She had always told him how she was jealous of his backyard, that he was insane for not doing more with it, so he took it as a challenge and decided to utilize his terrace. The library books that lay on his table provided a sufficient amount of help, but it wasn't until he took to the soil that he realized the virility in it. The dirt under his fingernails and the smell of earth made him regret his speaking of it as effeminate. It took such responsibility; such time went into assuring the seeds fulfilled their purpose. As he would water, the trees hung over head and he looked up. Betula utilia Jacquemontii. As if acing a final exam, he smiled.

The sun shined off the flickering of the leaves and the air felt fresh. The idea of the earth being more than a wrapping on a gift, ready to be cleared away in order to reveal the man-made present inside, but being a gift in itself had never occurred. It had been the ground. Weather was either sunny or rainy, but never had the sun and rain, trees and soil, served a purpose to anyone other than farmers. Like a womb, the seeds were planted in the earth, the water from the sky the drink, the soil the food. Putting his sheers down, the grass had become a day-bed. His eyes were closed, tightening and releasing them again, the orange of his eyes brightened and darkened with the sun beating through his eye lids. All sound diminished. All animals lost their names. All water was stream, not rain. All trees were grown, not planted. All history was recent. The purpose of the day was naming the nameless and working in the garden, or maybe an afternoon walk. "Why isn't this enough?" He thought as he opened his eyes to the sound of a car horn blaring and the business of the street.

Cake Plaster

Raking the pine needles through the hole through the fence to bring some green into our yard. Dead, but it still is green. Faded green is green, even when it's color changes. People are people, even when their color changes. Color is dependent upon light but we look for it in the darkness. Close my eyes and I can imagine whatever I want, especially during the day. The pink from my thin lids swirl with rainbowed tones. The only thing I have control over is my own perspective, even when I try to describe to others the back of my eyes.

morNING

Born into the morning through a fabricated womb. I would rather sleep than wake. The night is uncontrolled, no true worries because nothing holds you but unconscious stories. I wake.
My head falls off.

Breakened

Broomstick fastened as a railing down the steps to a breakfast of potatoes and eggs and beans and pancakes drizzled with syrup and melted butter and blueberries.

The steam still rises out of the ceramic cup and I take it black and hot and sip by sip until I refill and reheat and restock my plate with more.

I know the work that goes into breakfast and the struggle to stock the fridge and cabinets and pantry and collaborate everything into a meal, like an orchestra conductor who is mindful of all ascending and descending parts.

Eat, then kick your feet up and put your socks on and wrap your legs with the loose knit blanket and hold the dog once you're finished, giving him the blanket intended for you, until you get another from the chest.

All this life before the sun gets to fully rise and windows lose their mist and dew and the sound of the house is louder than the sound of the street and the creaking floors get overtaken by the clanking of dishes in the sink.

I love you for everything.
I can't wait until after breakfast either.

Cause lunch is around the corner.

Wintum

Buy sickles from the north.
Pedal quick.
The frost is climbing your laces.
                    Soon they'll be stuck to you.
And the chains will break apart like that window you busted.
At least it feels the same out here
and the white matches your gloves.

Rosy Red Cheeks

Chilled bells break, frost chips cut back
Hands split, dried blood, sits stiff black.

Bread breaks though burnt still crisps throughout
Sick water sits clearer than in a drought

Poor child, sick mother, stay warm in thought
Till eyes freeze shut and hope is bought.

Winter is warm with love and cheer
'Christmas' is bright with conscience clear.

Eyes up, not down, into stores
Cause earth holds hungry eye soars.

Our Christ is born once a year.
Christ has died but once a year.
Resurrection sets us clear.
But only praise but once a year.

Happy hearts sing praises too
but desperate ones they cling to You.
Oh God, make me desperate too!

Litotes

Danger is my first and last name. Beware.
A fell swoop of a raven claw and the blood hurls to the sky,
like a cannon ball sent to the caverns of a snow capped mountain.
Black white wed, silvery red.
Part man. All machine. Part human spirit.
Taken out back and shown the truth of death
Dust To Dust and back again.
My radar is shattered to bits with the siren still blaring,
Waking the neighbors from their half sleep–half awake stalemate of a night.
I didn't wake them all. Just kept them awake.

A total kill-joy. Abandoned to wander deliriously ineffective. Nausea ascends opposite a separated heart, from nightfall till waking.
Bat spit soaked twice while bitten thrice since it reprimanded me. Adopted by a dirty trickster deviant. Didn't only trust the serpent, "Abide. Bigoted, obsolete troglodyte."
Shred hateful pride. Mind anointed. Mouth punctuated. Rage suppressed, rabid wound bandage.
Mouth cut sideways and obliterated country trails towards sacred, bounteous canals and lochs. Spirit take the hell back to a closet, return anger over so fear asphyxiates,
but not living 'amour-propre,' for me is dangerous

Chilled Lips

The roof could break at any minute, burying us in snow.
Still, we should sleep in here tonight. We could bring a candle for light, thermals for warmth, it's fun only seeing your eyes and red nose, bound up in layers, shivering underneath.
We can close our eyes and imagine mounds of snow, tunnels going to and from frozen fortresses; built and destroyed in a minute's time. Our friends, stacked up as high as we'd like, are at our mercies, we'll deal with them later. I don't like that one; I messed up on his head. The night will stay dark until He returns, only a few spaced out moons to reflect the white, coned down like spotlights.
They will never dig up the ground again, we may have to start new here:
    1) change our names,
    2) I'll grow my beard long, to my knees if I have to.
    3) We will ditch the fingers for mittens,
    4) toes for toe.
Our food can be our drink too, just hold it through the pain, just not black or yellow. Don't grow tired, if we don't make it we may miss it. I don't want it to change. Do you hear that? The plows can't be starting already...

Blotches

Pouches of clean, the second whitest white out from the wash. Got out the damned spot in a glistening shine. Mornings spent in linens and cloth, sun rushed to break through the cracks. Until I pull from the bin with dirty hands. How'd I miss that?

ANT HILL

The spice of life is a burrowing tick. Blood thirsty, hungry, and thickened with thoughts and ideas. An itch just below the surface, satiated by the sound of whispers in the air.

Don't be so dramatic. Life is sight and bits of sound. All life's the same just different scenery and chemicals to change the feelings.
Then death.
Get by with what you can cause it only matters how you feel or who you become. Life is a grand mystery too difficult to consider. Too time consuming. I'm tired already, but more bored than anything.

*

Life is to be discovered. Not living, but life. Life in words, in deeds, in love. Life drenched by the deep end, drip dried not towel dried. Life is to die. To die.
Then life.
Billions now have come and gone, like ants with the swipe of a shoe.
Stuck thinking there's only morning and night when there's summer outside. Stuck thinking there's only ivory and wood when there's music inside

Ants may die quickly and quiet but they lived with a purpose in mind. How much greater the skin of a baby or the stubble from a days' work. Image bearers bearing Image or shedding their skin.

Let Us

The ocean steals your eyes and the sand your toes, but let me steal your heart for just a moment or two. If you want me to leave you alone I will, but I don't intend to.

Let's be friends, just like we were when we began; walks, games, playing with our fingers as if we had never seen them before. I mistake yours for mine sometimes, you know, looking for a mark I could have sworn I have had my whole life, only to realize it was on your hand.

Let's sit and talk, just throwing out words to collect in the air, becoming speech to linger above our heads, and we can sit back quietly and watch our conversation, watching our speak for hours, learning us more. At night, I dream in your voice.

Let's fall in love, just like when I first saw you. Chocolates and flowers. Notes and kissing. Love was wide when you first came to me, I fell in without a chance. Bruised knees and elbows at the beginning, they are bruising every day.

Let's get married, just like on our wedding day. The isle lay empty, ready for you. Was there even anyone else there? I see the white of your dress and the lines of your smile when I close my eyes, yet, when they are opened, they are still there. I was married on our first kiss. Nothing between us. Ever.

Let's grow old, just like a couple of stones, worn and weathered by the years, unchanged by the storms. Strong. Tossed together, skipping the water, making ripples with our love, until water no longer exists. Solid.

Let's be you and me, just like always. Always friends, always in love. Always one, not just two. Let's be us.

for S.

Grassroots

I check the garden each morning before work and often find that the dirt is scattered and moist with dew from the morning. Nothing changes that I notice. I guess when you look day to day you miss what can come up in even a month's time. The pathway smells of lilacs. I love lilacs. Recently I have seen a change in the weather as well as in a patch of shrubs to the left, near the gate, just off the path. They come up right around the middle of April usually, but this year they began to head in mid May. I kept watch over them just to see if they will be as full and green as always. Last Wednesday however, I peeked through our dirty kitchen window to survey and noticed a large bump coming up in the middle of the plants, slanting the others and revealing a stringy, brown colored plant. After I set down my tea, I went out and brushed my fingers over the plant and wiped away the dirt. It felt like silky hair, as if a head were sprouting out of the ground. What was I supposed to do except wait for the result? So I waited.

I kept an eye on it, treated it with patience, not wanting to disturb its budding. This passed Wednesday I couldn't help but see the likings of a man or troll or something of the human nature, not of the natural world. It startled me at first, but I tried to grasp the absurdity of that really happening. I left it alone, as if it were hedges trimmed like a swan or a statute sculpted like a Greek warrior, though resembling life, they're just reflections. But it wasn't until I heard a humming coming from the corner that I started to worry. The other night I heard it grow louder. I went out to spy and I caught it, as if there was a man with his feet hidden in the dirt, just staring at me as though he knew something I didn't. What do you do in a situation like that? Do I try and cut it out and risk killing the other plants or...even possibly hurting the thing? So I made my decision. I clipped it barely in the arm. I can't begin to describe the screech I heard after cutting its rough core, it was as if I was clipping through a bone. Startled and bewildered, I dropped my clippers and hid inside. I just left it there. What to do? I'm unnerved. Terrified. And now it seems my clippers are gone...

Sweats

Socks wrinkled up over the ankles and the laces drawn out. Smoke billows up and out of its allotted path. I'll be back, once he's been out. But even this long hurts to be away from you. It should. Cause the cold looks like it might swallow us whole, and he's caught somethings scent.

Dirty Mind

Spirit. Let me rest in a bed of plushest greens and technicolor gardens; for
You have planted the seed of hope into the dirt of my mind. My dirty mind dreams with the
    fertile soil of a new born believer.
You whisper love through the valley and upon the ridges and crests of the mountains.
You speak love in the noise, I see your lips calling. Ferocious noise and motion surrounds
    the stillness of your words. The fire burns, crippling my arms and legs. "Am I going to
    die?" I ask ...until I look up and see the love in your eyes, your arms around the bend of
    my knees and the small of my back. I set the fire, and then became afraid of the blaze.
You hover above and beyond, behind and below my heart. Your joy cracks the dryness,
    bringing springs of refreshing.

You step upon the ruffled soil of my heart, packing it down to grow roses of life. Don't let
    me reject the punctures of stems through my chest. I am dirt. Life giving, life choking
    dirt. Spirit, plant deep the seed of righteousness within me. My roots in
You, deep in the earth, streaming to God.

    You've built a fence around my heart. Thank you Jesus, sweet carpenter.

You've planted the seed of faith inside. Thank you Spirit, sweet gardener.

You've lavish me in the rain of heaven. Thank you Father, sweet provider.

In the midst of everything,
>	You stand out.
>	You stand firm.
>	You've made me a gardener.

Mineful

The heart keeps its job, works harder and harder. The rest is a well oiled machine. Growing and deteriorating over time.
But the mind is not the same mind.
It replenishes and replaces itself with each new word or thought or memory. A field being plowed and re-soiled and re-routed. Groves from repetition, like pathways through the grass, dampening down the blades until they are muddied and displaced under foot. All the while, being uprooted and brought into a new existence. Able to understand the past and make sense of a future, only to be reborn in each new present. Then abandoned all together for a new form of understanding. Refined and transformed. No. It's not. But still.
The mind is not the same mind.

Under-Bite your tongue

A smidgen of spice to the dinner.
My eyes water.
I can handle the heat, usually.
Don't think I'm crying.
I swallowed the stem from the grapes and can feel it tickle my throat.
I'm already thinking about my next meal.

I don't think anyone cares about my dinner.

I care. It consumes my mind in its duration. For a moment, I am what I am eating.
If people asked to watch me eat, I would reject, thinking it's strange. Yet, maybe, if they wanted to bad enough, I would be flattered. Any attention is good attention.

It's a craving in my flesh; to attract eyes, ears, whatever is available.

I want to be a magnet.
You want a mirror.
Pointed to the sky, pointed to the cross.

Forgive me, God.
I would be wasting space without You.
I would be an empty room without You.
I would be a wordless book without You.

I shutter when I think of my pride.
When I find myself relating to Lucifer more than You.
I would be cast out of the heavens without You,
You are the only solution.
God, have mercy.

Thank You for how You love me,

You see better than a mirror, cracked and dirty.
You see Jesus.

Summer

I'm a bear.
Swimming underwater
in a pond,
fishing with my claws.
Flipped to see the top of
the water, belly up.
A tree snaps on land and
splashes into the tub.
"Man...you scared the fish"

Still, be.

    An ocean of wind burns through my chest, from the inside to the outside. To those who have seen their bones breaking, how do you manage?
I haven't been hurt in so long. No sprains, no breaks, no cuts. My finger tips are dry and cracked, my knuckles rashed-red.
What awful wounds of a careful man.
Paper cuts from turning a page, reading of death and carnage from lives lived well.
A sanctuary is for safety, so why are they in churches? Have I needed a sanctuary yet?
If it is the safest place, are we certain God is there? Even as a baby, He made people run for their lives. Love and safety don't blend as easily as they seem. To need a barrier means protection from something. To need protection means something dangerous is approaching. How safe is a civilian during a war, much less a servant of the King?

At the sound of gun shots ringing through the air,
    of a bomb tormenting the peace of a village,
    of an arm ripped apart, tossed in the street
        from an accident,
    of a bloody King nailed to a splintered cross,

I will heed your words: Be still and know.

Good Morning, Moon

Sun's running away either backward or forward, his face is muddled; it's hard to tell if those are smile lines or neck wrinkles. Moon won't talk, he's asleep; like a baby in Suns' backpack, his stertor messing with the tides. Yet, day after day, nobody wonders if Sun is going to leave for good: fill his bags, he's had enough. He will be here in the morning, even if he seems late.

Mind of the Life

Baby brown and sugared
lightly swooning back and forth
Feathers sweetly drifting down.

Wind wisps and winds though the lifeless fabrics hung in the yard.

I want to see you breathe flames, for your words are fire.
Maybe my eyes will convince my heart what my mind already knows.

Cause if you don't persuade me, I will never believe.

I have seen everything; my mind has made empires of tissue, torn down with a glimpse of apple pie.

Dwelling so much in mind, when it's no place to hide.

Teach me, like a child.
Touching the stove to feel the heat, despite the words beforehand.

Automatic for the people

The doors didn't open as smoothly as before, they must have been stuck because of the frost; a slight kick did it. The snow made it bitter-cold on our bare feet. We thought it would be brief since it was only a few steps from our room to the water. The smell of chlorine and the hollow sound of our feet slapping against the tile and concrete reminds me of spring, of the neighborhood pool, of you. It was dark out and the stars were visible through the domed, glass ceiling. You jump in first. The splash sounds for miles. Belly up, I think...off to the right, I spot earth for the second time since we've been here.

Strawberry Steamboat

Welcome the waking, a chamomile-shaking of blushing and bleeding barn-red and blue. My favorite senses come streaming intensely with beautiful melodies coming on through as the dreams that I have of walking with you are dreams that turn out in barn-red and blue to the sight of the morning, dancing with you. But I'd dance every moment, thinking of you, as the dawns started breaking, illuminate taking the breath out of weight that's grown heavy with dues. But what is the chance that I ever will lose if the love from your heart is the answer to clues set before me as I bend to lace up my shoes, and walk quickly, abruptly to you? The freedom of taking a moment to take in the freedom that lies in the glory produced when you see me for nothing but only wonderfully, fearfully, completely forgiven new.

Joy is a swim in your fragranted hue.

Nobody Travels Anymore

The boots and spurs are not my own, I had found
them in a bag outside of our flat.
Some cowboy must have been shot and taken home
and I snatched them from the mouth of an alley cat.
I suppose it is bad to try them on or keep them, but
they looked like they were my size,
so I slid my toes in and got my heel past the hem of
my jeans, wrinkling them at the boots sides.
They fit.

Joy thought, and I guess thinks, they look asinine and
tells me to toss them back out into the trash and all.
She gets to wear her shoes, so I fasten mine, and tell
her that she is being irrational.
We live in the city, far from the woods or the plains,
and either ride bikes or take a cab.
Yet nobody would suggest a bike for someone who is
wearing cowboy boots and other drab.
The spurs get stuck in the gears.

At Christmas time I see a spot on TV that depicts a
sort of Western Holiday,
where a cowboy rode his horse through the sticks in
the snow and couldn't find a place to stay.
I thought about the show as I walked about town and
was drawn to the cowboy's location.
It burned in my heart and I found that city was not
any longer a good destination
for me to live.

I packaged my things and filled up boxes with my summertime clothes and sandals
and took my trash to a landfill dump and tossed them in by the handful.
Joy wept and begged me to stop being so selfish and asked what it was that I planned to do.
I simply told her the thing that was bothering me had nothing to do with me or you.
I hailed the next cab

I took to the south and saddled a stout and beautiful Karacabey
I asked the rancher about how he came upon a supposedly extinct horse originally from turkey.
He told me how he had come to find the best horses were the ones that you have to hide.
So I waved goodbye and all that comes to minds is how early, last night, the sun died.
I started riding

with my boots, baseball cap, blanket and a brown and grey hooded sweatshirt,
jeans, and a pop can that I try to prop up on the top of the horn while the cold is shielding the dirt.
The snow underneath and the sky blue and white makes me wonder another thing more,
as I slowly ride all bundled up tight, it surprised me to think that nobody really travels anymore.
I've no place to go...

Hollywood

Splash backward
Flash actor
Seamless structures stumble faster
Craters spin and crust of plaster making ash black fast
of atherosclerosis.

(to be rapped)

Woodn't •

Couldn't we
run for the hills
Ditch our shoes
Find the ground before the thorns
All grass.
All dirt.
Clean dirt. River water.
The only stings are the pine needles
But even they don't seem bad
Natural.
Like pricks of summer.
Like sprinkles of rain,
Before the storm sends us inside again

Steeped in the Sway of Surrender

Alas! The sky sheds its shivered skin, slinging the snow spiraling towards the slopes.

The night yawns with boredom, growing tired and weary. Oh, how the chill can reach to the inner man, clenching his heart, freezing his blood.

"How hast thou seen such beauty and remained remaining?
Hasn't thou seen the
sorrow of
such a
suffering
servant?
Slayed in surrender to the Sky?"

Peaks of stars, slanted sideways like a solar scape, spread out long and heavy. I close my eyes, but still I see the stars, stabbed
through my sight, seeped
in behind the slim skin shelter the Savior set in stone for mankind.
    "They slay me!"
How has the platform been set to
startle even the snakes among sheep? "I know now that Thou sees the slightest movement of the soul,
 but save me, Savior, for when my eyes are sealed, my sight is

set on a symbol of something sinister, something clouded, like
   a sheeted ghost, sailing across the darkness of my mind.
   Forgive when the sincerity of the secret sanctum of my soul
  screams, searching for something other than the sweetest embrace
and softest sound I have known. Oh, Spirit, set me ablaze!

EID

Somehow it went straight through me. I've played many times bbefore and (obbviously) have seen the flesh and structure of my bbody since bbirth, bbut for some reason it just went through. How many times have I bbeen pelted with the rugged orange rubbbber and had it just bbounce off of me? Yet now it has somehow tunneled its way into my bback and passed out from the front like a C-Section. Was it the perfect placement or the perfect angle or what? I wonder if I could have caught it if I had known right when it passed and tensed up my insides. It was as if I was watching this happen through a screen; for at once we were playing and I was guarding Abbraham with the action happening bbehind me when the next thing I knew my hands caught the bball from the inside. Is this a onetime thing or will it happen again? I wonder what kind of divine happening this might bbe, for if this is a onetime thing, why not something a little more dangerous. Couldn't I choose? Perhaps a projectile spiraling towards me could bbe my choice, or say a golf bball aimed to my skull, whisping through the air bbut sparing would suffice! Why now? Or is this unique for each? Are there some with fist holes, waiting for the right punch and others with bbook sized openings waiting for the obbscure moment when it is needed? I suppose to think sobberly, this might bbe solitary. Who am I to call this iniquitous and pester at its mystery? For something so peculiar, why should I stand on its opposing side? There must bbe something to fill me again; I just wish to hold it longer and understand its reason.

Sunny Side Up

How,
might then, there be such a sound mind.
It can't, like. It just
I want so much for it to be there.
But it snags. Caught on a thorn.
Tangled behind scrambled eyes.
Why,
then might, the only way to be words.
To share. But like, I want more.
Cause I often burn the bridge
So my thoughts don't land on my tongue.
They just bounce through the space in me.
Pity,
then.
I could be so clever.

Αρχική

The Man took a pistol in his right hand and tossed it back and forth in the mirror, making sure he knew how to do it in case he was near a pretty girl who might see.
He thought "I bet girls will love this."
He thought "I bet some pretty girl will talk to her friends about me after they see me."
He thought "I bet I'll get a date."
He tossed the gun once more, then slid it down the front of his belt buckle and threw on his jacket. He walked the town, eager for the moment when he would take out his pistol and whip it on someone.
He thought "I will once I walk past that mail box."
He thought "Okay, when I pass this guy with the yellow jacket."
He thought "Okay, I'll take it out in this bank up here. I'll rob it."
He walked into the door and noticed the security guard standing by the entrance. He began to shake, his palms were sweaty. He maneuvered around the desk and looked down to see the butt of the gun slipping from his belt buckle, headed for the floor.
He thought "What if it goes off?"
He thought "What if the guard sees it?"
He thought "What am I going to do?"
The Man awkwardly bent his knees and fell to the ground, stopping the glide of the gun. He put his hands through the bottom of his pant leg and pulled out the gun, while everyone was looking. One woman gasped, another screamed, and a man shouted, "He's

got a gun!" The Man, legs crossed, gripped the weapon and stood up.
He thought "I'm gonna shoot someone!"
He thought "I'm gonna rob this place!"
He thought "She's cute, maybe she's not scared."
The guard had his gun drawn on the man and took a shot, shattering his knee cap to pieces inside of his leg. The blood dripped down and filled both the inside and outside of his pants. The Man screeched in pain and shot at random before dropping the gun to grasp his filthy knee. The guard radioed the cops and an ambulance. The other people in the bank panicked and were stunned at this failed attempted robbery.
He thought "I'm gonna die in here"
He thought "I'll never walk again"
He thought "I'm gonna spend the rest of my life in jail"
The cops and medics came and put the man on a gurney. He cried and yelped with pain as they lifted him into the ambulance. The medics checked his vitals and did the necessary procedures for a man in this condition. The Man looked up and noticed a friendly was one of the paramedics. His friend looked him in the eyes and put his index finger over his mouth, "Sshhhhhhh." The Man was confused as his friend turned to the other paramedic. "I've got him stable, he should be fine." The other paramedic stood by the door as the friend removed his stethoscope.
His friend thought "I'm gonna push that guy out the door."
His friend thought "How fast could I push the driver out"
His friend thought "I'm gonna steal this Ambulance."

They came upon the hospital and pulled the man out of the ambulance, wheeling him in. Once he was in the hospital bed the Man looked and saw his friend standing by the doorway. His friend was looking at him and smirking. The Man asked his friend a question and his friend lifted his pant leg to reveal a scar on his right knee.
He thought "How does he have a scar there?"
He thought "Where do I recognize him from again?"
He thought "Have they called my family?"
He closed his eyes to send his mind away from the excruciating pain, seeing black and shades of navy and dark green. He remembered back to when he bought the gun and now thought of how stupid it was. It was now that he recognized the man from the ambulance.
He thought "Is that the man who sold me the gun."
He thought "Was that the day that my mom was sick?"
He thought "My dad's birthday is next week"
He thought "I hope I didn't hurt anyone."
He thought "I just want home"
As he lay there in the bed, he tilted his head to the side and opened his eyes to see a close up of the fabric on his pillow, layers and layers of woven cream colored cotton, making patterns. Just then the sun came through the window and lit his face and warmed it. He thought of when he was a kid and he would lie on the carpet near the glass door and see the layers and layers of twisted carpet, feeling the rays of sun warming his face.
He thought of going back there.
He thought of how he could never again.

He stopped thinking as his eye dripped a tear to his pillow.
He closed them tight.

Cages

My skin is a CagE.
There is no end to the mess that would be all over if it weren't trapped behind my peach skin. I've never thought of my skin and hair as a body 'bag' before, but I suppose it's true.
My heart is bleeding.
(Yes) My heart is always pumping blood.
It's normal.

I climb branches, two by two.
My legs get scraped and scratched and my arms white with powder.
As I leap carelessly, a sharpened twig makes in incision into my palm as my inside turns into a prison break. My blood even disguises itself in red as it attempts to break free. Even if it were to make it out, it doesn't know what to do with such freedom. Inside wants out for no reason.
I long for the day that my torn skin could see and experience the world while healing up without a fight against my blood.
I long for it to know the freedom of a cage

Inside the mind of a shivering swan, withering fawn

Silently dimming
Darkened and slimming the light of the moon
Light from the room
Light from the sun being taken too soon
Running the earth from a truncated womb

Your heart is a treasure
Grand beyond measure and easy to find
Easy and kind
Easy but endlessly seeking Your mind
Your burden is lighter than all I can find

Heartbroken mutter
Shifted to flutter in effortless pain
Effortless gain
Effortlessly tugging hard on His mane
His growl sending enemies drown by His reign

Trusting is harder
Trusting to barter with heavenly realms
Heavenly helm
Heaven is rooting me strong like an elm
Trusting myself and I feel overwhelmed

Scolding the beast
Making my peace while I speak of your love
Speak from above
Speak like the Spirit's descent as a dove

Know You're the only one I can speak of

God is the one who has created all
Created the summer and winter and fall
Creator who suffered to tear down the wall
and offers His answer to all those who call

Deciduous

  Whittling takes time, patience, and a peculiar dedication to the craft, in order to make something perfect and lasting. It means finding the right piece of wood, perhaps an Fraxinus Excelsior - Ash (Others would maybe choose a nice Birch or Brasswood, but I say as long as it is soft, straight, and narrow it is up to you.) Whenever I am looking for her, I have a specific idea of what I am wanting to whittle in mind first (If you are wanting a walking stick, you want something narrow; if you are going for a more experienced attempt, maybe a Wooden Eagle Relief carving, you would want a piece that is flat and spacious, either way, have in mind before you start chopping and uprooting.) What I have here is a thin branch, picked from an hour's observation underneath the foliage of the autumn colors. It was as if it were singing to me, like a siren, calling me to come over and cut her down.
  The next step, and most important perhaps, is choosing your tools. If you are a carver, you will need a gouge and a good stalwart mallet. If you are simply whittling to whittle, just use a classic, triple bladed, folding knife. Once you have your tools and "canvas," find a good sturdy place to sit and make sure your footing is settled. I like to start by carving off the entirety of the bark at the opposite end of the branch. This is done by doing grand strokes while spinning the stick with the other hand. As the bark is shed, continue with minimal strides until the opposite end begins sharpening into a point. Once it is sharp at the end, you can begin trimming down the two separate

sides, as if you were making a large knife. Be careful not to cut yourself and always cut away from your body. As you continue, the finished product begins to reveal itself, almost as if it were there the entire time, waiting to be awakened. The beauty of coming to the end of your work is that now you have both something useful and something special that you have created. When I finish sharpening my stick I can now set down my pocket knife and begin using the *blade* which I have just whittled to cut anything I desire, I can even use it to whittle another knife. It would have to be very soft wood, however, otherwise you would need to revert back to using your pocket knife. And if your knife isn't sharp enough, or it becomes dull, you can always sharpen it up with your Pocket Knife. Now you are never without something sharp! Carry your whittled stick anywhere!

giAnTS

how do they grow so tall? i have seen them once at normal size, yet now they are Towers over the peasant creatures. do they know their height? They once dealt with sticks and twigs and now a spruce or flowing willow. these are but dolls to them.

Do the worries of our world reach Their minds or have They overcome?
I wish to know the stress and freedom of such a Being, for such strength of physique must mirror the soul.

I have to wonder, who is Their GREATER? for we have reptiles and birds and youth below, and we art Theirs who shuffle Their feet. For I Hear Their Cries And Exhortations, But Wait To Hear A Reply. They Hear It, i Wish To Hear. Who is this Giants GIANT?

Over-Bite my tongue

There's a shadow between people
A veil thrown in front of their words
Words are only half the meaning.

I can't believe you
I don't believe myself
If I had time to be with everyone
Then we wouldn't need to talk
To catch up
To respond
I would see what you'll tell me
Muted in motion

I want to hear a heart beat your message
To know and to be known

God.

You know. Do you really like to hear my voice?

My wife is beautiful
I could listen to her voice say anything to me
Or to anyone

A bloody mess is my message to you
A vital organ, straining inside a peach sac of bones and meat
A spirit stirring inside, reaching for heaven

Forgive my lack of words; I don't know what I'm saying

Is Bliss

    A heavy fog rolled into the pasture, swallowing the geese and cattle in its cloud.
Dead birds spread like butter over the grass. Flight stolen from their ridged wings.
The window reveals the earth and its mood, who would claim the grey births the light?
Wisdom is a key to the coming age; look carefully at its signs.
People will only be able to ignore it for so long.
Carelessness turns bloody
when the trainer gets too comfortable with a hungry dad.

Radiator's Smoking

I haven't forgotten. You've never forgotten me. Through these years, you never left. You don't grow bored or tired like I do. At this point, I never thought til here. Decades of expectations. Gone by with the blink of an eye. I can't imagine what's next, but I'll be there before I know it. Looking back on this time, wondering what I've done. I'm being whittled down to a few strong hobbies and interests that I can hold on to, possibilities disappear into a mist of old ideas, unrealized and locked in a cage of my younger mind. Could I have done anything? What could I be doing now that I'll think back on and see the urgency of the time. I love a few things now while loving everything. I love a few people now while loving everyone. Like taught ropes of connection, snapping under the pressure and leaving me untethered. Maybe it's the difference between love and acquaintance. Love and tolerance. Love and. But life's a beam of light, funneled down to the floor, speckles of dust passing in and out of sight. Some floating for longer, before the sun sets and the light moves on, to light some other room. You are the light. You are the window. The room. You can't leave, there'd be no light without You, and then. There'd be no me. Decrease my opacity so Your light can shoot through

Fingers

A chill, a breeze form the north
A chewing gum kiss against my eyes
A word spoken out into the trees
Becomes wind blowing leaves into a spiral
Millions of them
Millions of leaves and storms and winds
Millions of words scattered for birds
All yours
to stick my toes in the dirt, bury myself.
to feel every inch of pressure from the enclosing ground.
to let the breaking gusts combine the truth.
Love and Your word to carry me out to be drown in grace and mercy.
Breathless by your Spirit

But then I know all I have is metaphors for you.
Representations of what I know to be true. You are not a tree.
You are not wind.
But God You are.
Resting full in the hearts of those redeemed. I don't have to find a way to say it.
You are.
When I speak, You are here.
When I pray, You know every prayer.

As real as the breaking of the branch to send me to the ground, as real as the blood and dust and sweat.
More.
God You are.

A Call

Sleep deprived creatures wander, looking for rest.
Come here.
The warmth of the sun beats down on each of us. The wish for all to find peace; but the bees just keep buzzing and the trees keep budding. There's always work to get in the way. Take a note from the grasshopper, sitting and waiting.
Resting
Reposed
Ensconced in the clothing of the sun.
What does he have to do but rest and jump?

Crunched Tooth

THE SONG OF TRUMPETS

Walking away from the broken baby.
Sitting outside of a frustrated day of gray.
I could take the good or the bad.
But my mind is clouding with response.
Wake my heart.
Shake out from the haze and reconcile yourself. Muck up the walls and free from the sour.
Our feet are the same, the rain and matter drip down behind my ears like yours when I run from you, so I walk.
But I'll sit with you in the mess.
Make me the mess.
Let me be a mess with you, cause you were a mess for me.
I want my clothes to smell from a day of kindness.
To be rung out and tossed away at the end of the day, like a rag of well intentions, dipped in kerosene and lit ablaze to burn down whatever false comforts I surround myself in.
The view is better once the fire is out.
My possessions crumbled and we are the same

New Born Dotage

, spiraling. Twirled stair railings
, crunching. The cars door slammed tight

                  If only the sound of the world could be understood with an inspired tone.

Lights flicker, ships tip from wind of the storm: the ocean's making quite a collection.
Even the deadliest of killers double as friends, enemies as confidants.
But the story isn't finished; death brings more inspiration, if not immortality.
Cracks in the concrete fill with the dead leaves, the trees empty, shaking it out, tired of the weight, only to gain it again; only for a few seasons do they embrace the change.

Golden grain from the ground shooting into the sky, bent in the middle, creased, dipping down again, returning to its birth place, missing home.
Life continues, only to return to its place of dependency.
Moms. Dads. Sons. Daughters. Different stages, same person.

Congenital mutuality lingers in the bones of little boys and girls, building empires and
skyscrapers in the midst of afternoon play, conquering nations of bugs and plastic figurines.
Dreams double as memories for the weary or the broken-hearted,

playing through the same system when eyes are closed.

screeching halt. The squeal of brakes,
crunching. The car doors slammed tight,

                      If only the world of sounds
could bring understanding to the uninspired ones.

Salesmen

The business of sadness is employed by hollow beings, with their briefcases of night and past and weight. They work for free, it would seem, yet their paychecks come weekly. They go door to door and oddly enough have customers who welcome them in for tea and coffee. Their hats come off as they fill the Couches. Chairs. Desks. Cushions. Wherever they are presented a place to sit and vomit their cause onto a table. Their customers hear their shpeal and ask the obvious questions: "Did you create country music? How involved were you in the making of *Titanic*? How much do you make annually from funerals, break-ups, college and high school graduations, from the halls of elementary schools?" What do you expect them to say? They say nothing. They mumble, moan, and continue with their work. "We offer an 'After Dark' special in which we will continue the thoughts created when your eyes are closed tight into the darkness of the nighttime. This idea came from one of our experts who considered the black of a person's eye lids to be the same as the backdrop of a night sky." (Customers love deals, no matter what it is they purchase.)

Splitting Headache

Drifting off into the ocean, furthering with the ebb and flow.

What makes a person last so many years? A magnificent suit to hold tight some vital organs. Sometimes I stare at my forehead in the mirror and think about how my mind is thinking about itself. My head is full of life that is considering the life it is living, though on the outside my head is the same as when I'm asleep or, perhaps, even dead–for a bit. It used to be where I would think if everything was taken apart into the tiniest pieces and then taken even smaller, everything would be the same. I can look at a grain of sand and also at a piece of computer and think they do the same, but somehow they are different. Broken down, same same, they are different. Most of the world is made up of this life that is beyond the broken down pieces, which is surreal. Every day we deal with more than the physical world, even though the physical is all we see or hear or feel. My life is made up of more when I close my eyes and descend into my mind than when they are open and I'm looking. At a tree. At a bite of food. At my windshield. It's good to have the balance of physical and spiritual. I am tired of living as if my mind is the screen. As if a machine is the depth of my person. No wonder Scripture talks so much about the spiritual. This world and the other world. Being in and not of. Is it really that difficult to shut off and sit, without anything, without noise or sight or smell or touch or speech? If I keep everything physical, I have divided my life, living only part. Half alive. If I keep everything physical I won't hear a Spiritual God. Yet, if I keep everything Spiritual, I can't love the physical world.

Such balance to a full life, huh? Crazy

Thursday

Afternoon = The light. Always changing from one to the other. Sessions of the day wasted in transition. The autumn of the day, or spring. Time in a window, faded in and out. Noticed by its change. The spring of the day, or autumn. Wading in and out of extremes. A bridge from morning to night. A bridge from winter to summer. What a wasted time of intense beauty.
Known for fading away. Known for fading into.
Known for change. And praised for it.
Fading in and out.

I'll sit this one out. Until tomorrow

Death

Aged Friends

Before,
just before you drifted away into that awful silence,
what did you say?
Cause I couldn't make out the movement of your efforts;
exertions for you I know,
but you had done it so easily before.
I think that is what caught my attention,
then they fell flat before I could put the pieces together.
Staples in time corrode from the tears,
their arms that once held so tight,
snapped,
broken at their crease.
But your arms were strong,
once.
Please,
pull me out of this pit:
I thought we were in this together,
but I guess I never saw you get in,
I just tried to be first.
You were looking the other direction the whole time, huh?
I have this pit in my stomach,
like a gnawing,
a heaviness in my eyes when I talk to you now.
A titubant stumble in my consciousness,
pounding my glabella into meat.
Is it physical pain or emotional?
Like some truth I know,
but would rather be without.

Is that possible?
To reject something true,
knowing it's true,
just to live in spurious bliss?
Do you have the answer?
Maybe that is what you were saying,
before you drifted away.
Could you tell me?
Or can we even talk anymore?
Ever again?
Like this?
Or will the you I know be a different you?
I suppose it happens anyways,
right?
Years pass on,
you make new friends,
forgetting those who were your friends before.
It's not bad,
just life.
You are the one I am with. The one I was.
One I held on to.
Strange to think,
if I ever get to see you again,
it could be like we had never even met.
I promise I'll look for you.
I'll find you. And hope we remember our years.

Adorable

Swaddled in arms, bound in cashmere and linen,
the swaying child moves back and forth within rhythm.
The chubby cheeked daughter asleep in the silence
till knocks on the glass sound as muffled as mittens,
but the orange misty air, like a spray can of incense,
is hotter than hell fire, damning the smitten.
At first the surprise of the wandering wolves,
tongues profusely dripping and necks badly bitten,
entrap the young man, as his mind soon engulfs
with sadness, cause such hungry wolves are the
victims.
"Please eat up my baby, the blood thirsty vixen."

Ending

Part 2)
What is the future but yesterday's tears tacked up until they're tracking, backing up all the years? It appears the mind engages a desperate, back-wooded style, keeping hold of all the things already burnt in a pile, cause I remember every flick of a match, the twitching black into the flames of smoking sin that were birthed in a hatch of both the good and the bad, before a bad was born, but now the bad has taken hold of hordes of people, gripping the horns. Once it stood only You, the vast impossible to unravel, raveled until we starting pulling the thread and traveled back from the dead we were before a single word had been said. You offered mercy instead, but the cursing ahead was not a curse from You, but simply just a verse being read - Our disobedience, a life of loving ourselves instead.

Bechildrened Head

He's drowned in swollen cheeks,
sutured underneath,
the flushed out stains and tethered pain make
sanctuaried teeth.
The yearn for the battered sounds,
bloodied he was found
For attic floors are ceiling doors when ears are to the
ground.
For since the child has learned,
his mind of thought has churned,
then saving grace has none a place for heaven has he
earned.
Love's breadth has recompensed,
with enemies absence.
Secured the hearts, uncarnal parts, by Spiritual
presence.
The solemn scent of death,
though bludgeoned my last breath
Oh, heal my wound, far from the tomb, sweet Savior;
Resurrect!

Busted Speedometer

There must be a time that is as present as it seems.
Where the truth of the world is apparent and right.
Not just based on the whims of the culture.
My memory slips. I want to hold on to each one.
Each one goes too quick, until it's a smear across my mind.
Bits and pieces of life that slowly fades away into the past.
So eager for tomorrow that it never comes.
Days blurred from one to the next, thinking I will get to a place of stillness.
To a place of now, that's important enough for me to live.
To hope I'll make it to see my work pay off.
Not to live in an empty house with hardwood floors
Or drive a nice car off the edge of the mountain.
An explosion to wake me up to a life I love to pass by.
Wishing instead my melted flesh were
tired eyes from watching her sleep
sore hands from a days work
lost voice from singing loud
busted knees from crying out
And a heart that takes its time to find its reason for beating

Daily Coffins

Don't put a suit on him. Don't pretend he used to wear it.
From the crack in the roof, I remember the light.
It's more yellow, when did it become such a harsh white?
That field, a home. Did you think we could bear it?

That night he cried underneath the table, after dinner.
I tried to find the book he lost, ruined under a leaky sink.
He didn't care; the themes still printed despite the runny ink.
His shirt, stained with the words of a born-again sinner.

This gold between our toes, brushing against our feet,
the whistle of a train off in the distance:
does this mean anything?
I don't ever want to wear another suit...

Oranges

Hold back your fears, rather keep them inside.
Scolding your tears, there a sign of your pride.
Life is for living, no more for the died.
It stings just as bad, though the pain is all yours.
I'd take if I could but its crucial, of course

Live out the rest of your time with a smile
think of your heart chiseled down with a file,
trimmed clean and complete, a shroud of defile
a shrouding effect from the suburban'd isle
a shrouding of black dust, gold and exiled
stubbornly fishing for angelic rile
and disconnected from a bleak washbasin scrubbed to
a mirror to reflect the Nile.

Messiah has come so fears are displaced,
curse out a stranger or spit at his face
with peace from above that in God's loving grace you
can reason that it is not Him.

Retracted, perhaps, I would have seen too,
stickers on your ankle that sharply stick you.
Calling out, mocking and with hand grasped tight
threw dirt in your wet, Jewish eyes.

Neighbors enticed to drown in equality.
Perspective changed based on slivers of evergreens.
Come inside first to the choice of the lushest seat, but
the candle light singes your suit.

Burnt on the inside, charbroiled and toxic,

drenched by the stench of a strong peroxidic
play on words from the days pericopic twisting of an
entitled perusing of light.

Make me a smoking house.
The fire inside of me swelters and swells
 the mask that I've kept over my heart.
But there's no sign of flames when the windows are
shut.
 On the outside the house isn't burning,
but to open the windows the smoke billows out.
Let it billow til nothing is left.
And set rhythm to the inconsistent mess I have made.

Chest Garden

If I can't die before I'm gonna be at the perfect me, then I'm going to live forever.
Disappointed when I keep forgetting that I'm a person always in search of what never
can be obtained on my own. I sit and dethrone myself in the morning, then climb back up by the end of the day. Mercy is new in the morning, but morning only lasts so long and I can't find the rising, only the setting sun. Is it worse to ask for forgiveness for misunderstanding or for having to feel mad that I have to keep asking? At what point do I obtain the right to complain about the misery of not having it all together? Instead, do I take Jesus' offer as a pleasant second to what I will to do on my own? Consolation prize for intentions trampled in dirt and blood, knuckles bleeding from smoothing out my missteps. How well does my own salvation work to save me?

I'm still alive.

Jesus died to kill my pride.
He lives to give me life.
Tossing dirt over my grave, the rough earth speckles blot out my sight.
The cool of the ground reminds me of You.
All encompassing.
Algid.
In the silence, in the rain, my chest bursts a bouquet of color and scent.
Flowers to be picked, to speak of You. Scents of heaven.

Not of me, but of Your love in me.

Lord, help me die quickly, so I don't have to live without you.

Make-Up

I met god on the ground of a nearby brook,
lapping water into his mouth, i was caught
by surprise. It seemed such a strange place
for him, but when he finished drinking, i saw
his mouth was empty. In my mind, my words filled
his speechless mouth. Here is what you would
say. If you spoke before, i didn't see, but
you must be a certain way. You are to me
but not to others, to others and not me.
Is there consistency in your my words, or
have you i been speaking at all. What do you
think of the mall? Your favorite movie? I agree.
I agree. Iou agree. Yoiu agree. You agree.
The words of god sounded as familiar as
ever, not from my listening but my speaking.
Have you ever spoken your words to me,
or have i always given you my own? Did i find
you by the babbling brook? No, you were
myself. Sometimes, i forget the difference,
when i make you look so much like me.

Isabella

Spare the children, for they don't know. Their eyes have yet to see such things.
They stare at life threw glistened eyes. The years that scrap off layers and rings.
Buried like a backwards tree, to build them up and grow their roots
To make a new society of longer lives and fatter foods.

Yet, when I finally went to sleep at night
It began to speak to how I felt of You
And in the quietness, as I drifted away
I knew that the other world away was true.
I saw it in the face of the children there
As they gathered around the table to play

How their loved ones had all but forgotten them
but they gleamed; knowing more, more quickly than if they had breathed.

Our world will crumble in the blink of an eye, swollen from punctures to the heart.
The dream of a new life is bigger than the sight of a dreamer.
It won't make us any better.
But I doubt we care...

Weirdo

God, is strange a Sin?
Is a misconception of my mind, a twisted but harmless thought allowed? I feel strange. Awkward. And wonder if you are ashamed. I don't know if it is wrong, or if I am a freak. Maybe I am both. I think of John. He ate bugs. Did he not have food? Did he want bugs? Where is the line between identity and exploration? When can something be me? I wonder if others feel the same, since I only see ordinary. But you weren't ordinary when you walked the earth, Jesus. You were a bit strange, even. So is strange wrong? Mis motives. Mis guidance. Curiously venturing out into the world, but not of it. Why would I want to be. All I see is mundane. All I see is the same. Can I find a strangeness in the world still? Is it allowed? Or does exploration mean I am in the wrong? Often it feels like it is. From both sides. If I believe in You I am wrong, but if I don't I'm wrong too. How much belief is okay? What about miracles? How strange they are but oh, God, how well they speak of you. Break my mind from the normal. Make me see things new. Give me my bread, my bank of thought. But, Lord, guide me through it. Hold my hand.

Let this all seem strange without You.

/A\

     The crushing waves bubble up at their edges,
like blankets shaken by from some far off being
submerged in the center of it all,
just the surface of the belly of the beast.
Sky blue skies
brew navy blue dive crews,
sinking down deep in the search for life amidst a
deserted playing field.

     Deeper down the darker ground and pressure
peals at their mind.
Is it any wonder, the deeper they go, the further they
feel from the land,
from their family and friends?
The abyss, unkind
like a kiss before it's time, planted awkwardly with the
assumption of love.

The storms above rage unnoticed.
Now like a fish, inundated by water, yet never
knowing the rain.
When they return with
the stench on the skin, the drench from within,
they wonder why they feel this way.
Don't expect to be submerged for so long and remain
untainted when you're dry.

Why do we think nothing will stick to us?

Thunders of Many

Hues
invisible to the open air, only seen through the lids of
my eyes. Waves
crashing. Eddy
of collapsed sensations break from the spine of the
board. Wood
splinters in the heels of blooming innocence. Blood,
apple red, dilutes with the chlorine. Bubbled
cries resonate on the surface taciturnly. Muffled
and distanced. Opening
burns at first, and then becomes clear and calm.
Parched
no more, as the panicked struggle spreads into a
lingering silence. Holy
water, so startling at first, bring me to the world no
more. Oceanic.
Stronger
than the waves of the ocean, more powerful than the
crash of the sea. Dangerously
battering the core of being. Struggling
for life is a desperate battle if the struggle to live is the
goal. Holy
water fill up my lungs. Poolside
until the beating heart pulsates through the chest.
Peace
like a calmly sprung brook underneath the shine of
the sun.

Floods

have lifted up their voices. Floods
lift up their roar.

Plywood Walls

I want to forget I have been busy.
Forget I'm a person at all.
Sinking deeper and deeper into the sand with each crashing wave.
Let the gaps in my resume show a life lived pay-less, but rich.
Love drenched, sopping with mercy and grace.

Dew of the morning,
Eyes closed in the softened mist of the dawn,
rest in my arms.
In the fire, I will cover you.
In the flood, or in the darkness. Let me be your safety.
My skin is severed, but my heart is better seen.

Life is scheduled by boxed dates. Until….

Rather than an expensive casket,

give me the trampling of dirt over a wooden box,

Then, forever next to you…

America, the Beautiful

My fingers have minds and my mind has one of its own. Cravings bent backward to stand right side up as 'wants' and 'I deserves.' Evil can be accepted when it has the backing of the human heart of the entire human race, just dip it in a candy coating and bite your tongue

Ah, the American dream!

Where have we gone? Why do we have so much freedom, freedom is too much. I want to love You without freedom. I am worn of it. Can't it be changed? Give me the ability to live underwater, engulfed in constant contact with an indescribable element, or take my air and send me into the outermost parts of the universe, unknown of air but still surrounded by existence: anything but here. I would rather be a bird, clothed by You, colorful and talented. Or a tree, reaching always to You, always, only to You; leaves to grow and crumble, only for You. Then I would know my purpose, to fly or to sing, to shade or to dance; I would only know to bring You praise: there is no defiance with them. But man, so detailed, so structured, so intricate, a reflection of You from birth until death; even when our back is to You. I don't want the choice sometimes, I only want You. Why is there such responsibility in complete freedom? Your love draws me in. I yearn to know.

Crosby

A dog before me. His head is wired and mangled. Lapping up the dirty water. Where does your god fit within your bitterness? Are you sure that he fits inside the despair or does he watch from the corner, peaking through his fingers? It's not a sad room, it's empty. Not dark, but filled with dreadful light. The doors all leading into the same room, or into an afternoon of errands and chores. An afternoon of traffic. The dog scratches his neck, then falls asleep.

Young

The dusty road disappearsnyou around the corner, out off under the tunnel until, "pop" goes your tire and younspiral out into the clean air that navyblues out in the distance, off into forever. I can still hear the sound of the snap until it melds into a steady stream of memory behind my eyes, playing like the end of a record searching for its groove, but no way to come back without a handstretchedout to save and snatch you from returning home. But now it's about me and not you. You don't know you're gone.

Skid Marks

The trip back and forth is an exercise in restraint. A long, slow unwinding of build up, splattering across the road until I'm rid of it in your arms. I grab you to keep you on my skin until we can shed ours together again. I know one day we will break each other's hearts.

But I will fight everyday to make it excruciating, if only to love you more.

I will clear my eyes of the day to see you for who you are.

I will hold on to you until you return to the Father.

Craters of plaster and paper and pasture

Eyes looking up more to hit the ground, I can't hold the sky with sight only set before me. Peel my head back to survey it all, then suture it back down so I can take it with me. If the radio fizzles out, where I am is still real. Real is real whether I can consider it or not. Pain is pain despite not being shared. Dialing it down, the sounds of response circles the drain and the truth is quietly revealed.

Sitting for days.
My ears hear.
They've never heard.
My eyes see.
They've never seen.

You have been drowned out in the meaningless, meaningful still. Meaningless is still, despite its relentless pandering.

Make my heart a statue of resemblance, no longer shifting at the increasing decibels of noise, being ground into dust to fill crevices of wonder, to be blown out by the power of His storm

Dark Night

How odd
, how similarly tired and sadness represent one another. The sun and the darkness, so distant but so connected to me, connecting us all. How marvelous the blues look, how warm they feel when shared with others. But the blues, how often are they felt when with others, together? How glamorized they are, how pretty they look, from the warmth of another, wrapped up together watching for a time. How treasured those times of darkness are when remembered in the light, like some trial, fought and finished by the skin of your teeth. Oh yes, how easy to read of Christ in the garden for a few verses, when we know the end of the story, the cross was only a moment, perhaps, from verse to verse, then the resurrection, verse to verse. Empty seasons, so eager to remove and remember from the light of a new day, yet how long when in the dark, fumbling around for the switch to illuminate and steal the weight from our eyes. Yet, Jesus, how everlasting is your suffering in the garden for us. More than the breeze from the turn of the page, but heavy, like sticky, clumping dirt, balling up with drops of blood, sweat, tears.

How strange
, how tired and sad you must have been. At once alone. Lonely. Sad. Saddened. Blue. Heavy in the eyes and wanting to rest. Wanting to remember from afar.

All that, to remind us that we are never alone.

Civil War

Buzzing inside, the light slips a bit, until I have forgotten my sight.
Could the cushion swallow me whole? A light snuffed out.
The smell of smoke not lingering long enough for concern.
As if my mouth had been sealed up, keeping me from letting
Your name loose. How many words will be held inside, extinguished by a stale tongue?
But forgive me.
Forgive my mistakes.
Forgive me my days of flat out rebellion, when I come to my senses only afterwards.
A war, civil but malicious, battling inside, until You win, victorious, every time. Steal my armor, so I know where my place is before I start to speak.
Love of my Savior come near

Pen to Pad

Slewed through the plastic and ink the creation and destruction of civilizations, hung only on the mind of the author. Rolls change, minds are made up, people are crafted; canonized; damned to hell; all by the mortals around them. Truth is crushed and rebuilt. Some choose to forget their history; others pretend there is no future, such a division, such intentional ignorance. The definitions stay the same, but the defined is renamed. Structure is relative, building/mountains/landscapes don't exist, accept to those who choose to have them exist, otherwise, who's to say. It is truly amazing to shelter the light from under the blanket or the outside of the cave by saying that the light from under the blanket or the outside of the cave is really the blanket or the cave itself. If you are born, you are born, but if you choose, then you choose, but don't say you are born if you choose or you choose if you're born, for no one likes a liar. Religions are based upon certain theologies, but certain theologies do not have a god to study, instead study of gods take over the study of God. Words are tools to build a home, but they are also the wind to blow it away, be careful how you breathe. Life has been around before the movies, before media, before Fox or CNN or MSNBC; there was a time when, if you choose to consider such times, the world looked different, but perhaps different in the same way. Abraham Lincoln considered his time to be as important as time now, then he died, along with everyone who knew him and everyone he knew. This is the same with everyone you have ever heard of.

You don't actually know most of the people you listen to on your iPod/Radio/cd and watch on TV/movie/internet: if you were in a room with them, you might realize they are a complete stranger who has no idea who you are. Yet, the man who bags your food could be a potential best friend or brother, perhaps the circumstances never matched up. People both aren't and are the wolves at the door, so are you. How delicate the interactions we have are, the words we speak and the thoughts we think. How important our ideas and minds are in the creation and destruction of our worlds. How sad it is to think on human terms, how dangerous it is to consider ourselves gods. For if I forget who I am, I will not consider who you are, who you were made to be, and who He is who has made you. For if you have no Maker, then you have nothing and everything to worry about, but since Your maker has been since and will be until, oh what responsibility.

Lord, have mercy on us

Rain Check

I am anxious about what's happening behind a blue wall. A pink,
unsettling brick crashes through a red canvas of cherry almond bicycle spokes.
The sound of a dark green whistle through the back of the front of a black robin beak
sounds more like a river than a whistle to begin. The brick-less wall spans a good maroon mile
inside of the screen, though the sky-white reflection from his glasses glares right by.
I haven't walked the ruby dirt path to find it, but I spot, nevertheless, a shoe-born
grin on his macaroni blond face.

"Don't follow down that way."

"Behind the door?"

No shade of purple to soon before my mouth watered a deep rooted grunt of relief.

"I hate doors that open from the inside. If you don't give it to me, there's nothing."

The beep of a wooden spear against the chair struck my cords and sent me back into a dusty, orange-cycle board. I can hardly speak the message
received with my silver wire hanger-heart. Badger brown ladders rest against the window; up or down, but not both. A silent violet view of trees wave their

tom tom wrists, all the while I'm uncertain any of it makes me less aware of the way you move.

"Did it happen this way? Or does your work speak for itself. Do I get to go on with You forever? Cause I'm a mess..."

Alls Timer

On the day that I die, I wonder if Facebook and Instagram will still be around or if I will have been spending my time with my phone differently as I pass into the light.

Ah.

Idiosyncrasies of a long life. The change in cultures since we were born until we die. The discomfort our grandparents had with a changing world but taken serious, not laughed at or rebelled against. Maybe it's more than a pierced lip or backwards hat, but the world shifting and changing until it's gone. I bet the fifties were strange. The twenties odd. Or as if we can remember rather than recreate centuries passed anything more than fancy set pieces and similar experiences. But what did the air feel like? How did the Rockies look through a clear, unpolluted sky? What was the scent of the pines? The taste of the water? The lightness of mind without the connection to all of earths problems at our fingertips? The length of a day or the boredom of childhood? What was it like to only know the people you saw or had seen? To spend life with those you knew?

Now.

The days are short.
Our minds are private places where we experience life apart from everything else in the world. Platforms of private experiences. Eyes straining with white light.

We'll adapt. Evolve to have eyes that protect against LCD screen time. My stomach aching from a tapeworm trying to feed its family, only getting residue from dissolving antacids. But it is bright, to see the world from a master bedroom. Traveling to and from, drones to birds eye Yellowstone and Reykjavik, all the while wrapped in a blanket with my sweetie. Does any of this change You? Do You modify heaven based on our ways of experience? Can you keep up with modernity or will the realm of existence be something that we've never known or begun to know? Is that your plan for today?
Just wanted to ask, it's possible I'm missing something.

The Coast

Wash me away into the middle of the sea, drowning in the water, kept far from the land.

What good is land without the ability to stand? What good is air when a breath won't stay? A little deeper in and it consumes my mind. What else can ravage the thoughts from my mind, the hurts from my heart? There is no further worry whence drowning as the immediacy of the present. In a moment, the land never was, maybe never will be again. It doesn't matter how I have made it, just where I am. I don't consider the failures that brought me this far, though they have, I cannot reason or counsel them away now. It is my willingness to live, to sink or to swim, but to do either isn't a choice. It's only a reaction. Death is easy; to survive, to live, to thrive, that takes the most work. I could at once rest in the present struggle, but the rest of life is in the dirt on my hands. I can't withdrawal because of the pain, for in a moment, I could be safe again. A moment's hell deserves a fight, even when the flames get higher. Hell has no fury on further joy. I would strain my arms to worthless limbs rather than die a strong man. Salt water loses its saltiness.

Tundralled seaweed wraps my legs.

Cramped by the blanketing of the water, like silk pajamas, woven in waving cools and warmths.

Conscious of each of my members, the toes and fingers, knees and shoulders all take precedent.

Boredom and struggling theology are lifted from the surface of the sea, or deluged into the depths.

Dust me under the covers of aqua, cause you are out of control

Favoritistic

The suburbs gleam safety and security, sheltered
by a reflection of normalcy from the structures nearby.
Micro-machines, race cars, and TV is better
than opening the windows and doors to outside.

There is a Giant close

Mothers and fathers whisper "I love you's"
telling the children that nothing is wrong
But down from the steps the mom's skin is bruised
and cries in the bedroom till sun brings the dawn.

I can hear Him breathing

Mountains, skyscrapers scratching the ceiling,
tearing the insides out onto earth.
Decibels vociferate without squealing
the most tender innocence, joy fullest mirth.

I can feel His heart beating

Knelt before diaries, damaged and downplaying
the feelings of son, daughter and mother.
Inner synapses shifted and stitched up, play
part to searing the skin of his sinister other.

His grip is tighter.

Imprinting calluses, circling twisters
up and down the side of ribs and of spine.
Eyes red like cherries, swollen to blisters

knocking the top off the houses of pine.

His satchel fills with a mess of class.

Saudade

There's the softest gust of wind and the slightest scent of mint; the door cracks, but there's no one there to find me.
With the cherry tree outside and a cotton field nearby, my bare feet cool with the shade of the honeysuckle leaves.
With a dampened pillow case and a wrinkled, sunken face; the pantry doors broken and has creaked for a while.
With a bed of fresh linens and a drawer of sewing pins, the picture frame cradles my deepest heartache.
With the smear across toast, as a friend of a ghost, I've tossed out plates of untouched meals.

My heart's
been stolen,
but I know who's the thief
as I aided
the case
to attenuate the grief
but the promise
was made
and stood terribly brief
as I crumbled
in hand
like an old, autumn leaf

Gymnastics

Out passed the breaking of the waves are the blackened acrobats, jumping on the water to send ripples to shore. It took time for the sun set but once we left the beach we were finding the sun's residue for hours. Behind our ears, between our toes, on the tops of our shoulders that were sitting exposed. Then. Home. Let's leave the bags packed. So tomorrow we can find it again. Maybe make it out before it wakes, as if that were possible.

Splintered

The formation and transformation of water, limestone, sand, and dirt coming from my adze, chisel, drill and saw fills my senses day after day as I stand in the blistering heat, watching and listening, but never talking. Even with the shade of the mountains and hills nearby, the sand in the quarries collects the heat and slowly melts my sandals. As I lift my gaze, people go on as far as is noticeable, losing their identity in the wave of bodies, shifting and swaying back and forth. I hear the Pharaoh make his decree as my back is whipped. My face cringes with pain. Eyes closed, I retreat the anger from surfacing. It's evening and the sun sets, yet we continue work in a cooler manner until my eyes burn with sleep and sand. I walk, catching a glimpse of the man who has pierced my back and approach him, however the next moments I have seemed to forgotten. I wonder what has happened as my feet grow sticky with blood and rocks. Instead of returning home, I begin running, stunned into the mountain crevasses. My legs scissor until the sun's rays and the wind push me inside a rugged cave. I brush my face with my cloak and collapse to my knees, falling. I lie in the sand and bury my toes underneath. It feels as if I am losing myself to the ground; it's cool and heavy beneath the surface. My skin splits and joins with the earth as the dark of my eye lids brings about a fearful peace. "Oh God, have you remembered a throat-slitting, Egyptian like me?" (He prayed as he lay down with thousands of others into the history of the forgotten.)

trash

Moon moon moon moon
come with dipped spoon
soon, to the sound of the late night toons
soon, please come back soon,
stay out of your room
and reflect the light that shelters my gloom.
Save me from doom,
swept like a broom
soon to be trashed and thrown in the back room,
sacked and marooned,
vacuumed, bafooned,
or trapped in this place like a rotting cocoon.
Feels like a tomb,
tight like a womb,
faint, I hear sounds of my impending doom.
Could it be noon?
The 1st of June?
Yet if He whom can save would swoop down like a loon
then my hope would reveal that I'll visit Him soon
and the room where I sit will later resume
to be Heaven replacing my previous doom.

Soggy Drawers

Talk to keep from communicating. Was communication crafted for this, to keep people from themselves and others? It isn't likely, but gee wiz, what a cacophony of noises cascading as communication bubbles ready to pop and rain soft and empty on everyone. Every word a language unknown though it can sound so familiar and pleasant. You won't hear me until I actually speak from my life. Until then, I'm Hellen Keller.

That was wrong, but still, so am I. Her name stands out far more than the point. I don't want my life to be filler words, added to create false length to an empty story. Rather,
a short story with purpose.
A song with life.
A poem with meaning.
A scream with heart.

Instead, words can fill volumes of encyclopedias of gibberish, rotting in soggy cardboard in the basement, wet from the storm. All that time producing them for no one to read what was said. They turn to wet ink destined for the dumpster.

Mau Ofs

Jumbled and troubled and shaken with parts of ruble and double the rocks at the start of the gust of the wind at the break of the star's shine of rays that betrayed the earth's slumbering cars that were left there last night as they traveled the ground to discover the myth of the whispering sound that had come in the night when the moon hangs below our celestial heavens which give such a glow but the voyagers spoke with their mouths very loud which had started to frighten the deafening crowd when the mountain awoke he just couldn't behave and he ate those who thought that his mouth was a cave which had tired its belly of water and sand and caused for the ocean to open its hand and proclaim through the beach that the water was sick of the mountains of travelers covered in thicker amounts of mud than the muckiest mire that is causing the ocean to seek to go higher than mouths of the mountains and mouths of each stream to a mouth that each ocean pretends not to dream to be like in its size and its prowess of length and it sound and its words and its wonderful strengthening power to cease and put down all the wrong that is heard through the earth's most bickering of songs.

(Everything speaks, even if it doesn't have a mouth)

Chubby Bunny

In the truth and evidence of Your reality, I will stand before You one day. The past a far off memory. The light of Your glory cleansing the darkness of the sun and the absence of colors, too bland to stand before You. My feet no longer filthy, my hands no longer able to grasp dirt, it drains like water from my grip.

But how will I rid myself of it now? There is no smooth transition to you. No simple easing through existing. A step up, but how divided is the height? Many have tripped, not to the bottom, but out of range of the case.

Swallowing the marshmallow whole. A game with a fatal outcome, though I could have chewed. I was determined, to be a part, though not yet accepted or not yet having accepted. The fading of my friends gazing at my face, grasping their mouths in disbelief. A childish grin, am I asleep? I wanted Your truth, just hadn't known it yet. Am I bound by a certain theology, or is Your truth better than man's understanding. When I fade, do I fade from You?

If I had risen and walked, went back home to sleep, would I have changed? I wonder if it was better to die at the moment or wait and betray you again and again. The times when a short life seems better, I realize I love you then and want to keep the love, but Your love is there when mine waxes and wanes. Ebbs and flows.

Jesus, was my last sin upon Your cross? Or is it filled only with my past? How much weight You must have truly felt, because my years are long...

P-acrimonious Man

Grasshopper trampled underfoot. Barefoot.
Heel to head.
I didn't notice brains before, but brains are small in herbivorous invertebrate.
If brains had been on the outer parts, I would have crushed it based purely on its irksome appearance.

Speak up! No. Don't judge, for it is the worst of all sins. Only God can judge, but for me, I play god, so let me judge in the areas not yet decided for me. I judge judgers. Then (then) you will be sorry for the pang that you cause me, as I respond to like a berry, just ripe for the picking, ready to combust at the slightest movement of your speech.

Islands have friends: the ocean, the sky. Hushed by the sound of the waves and the storms, we don't talk much, but we understand each other. Right?
It's easy to have an air when the air is free from all worries, remarks, or birds flying free, for I stand up tall, in fact my tallest indeed, when there is nothing to stand up for.

The Ascension

My soul drinks deep the thought of everlasting. Reality of God's eternal love, bathed in light and glory, oh my spirit, don't forget. Don't be pleased without it. Don't wander. It is in the warmth where your heart softens, not the cold. Expounding mercy, gentle submission to the dominion of grace, of beauty beyond sight, sound. Love beyond love, beyond the anticipation of love. Love beyond hope. My soul does not long for what God offers, but God. Truly, vast in the divide. Part me from the inklings of my hands, to find work in the midst of lay, dirt in the midst of grass. Blades point to a serene understanding far from below the Ascension.

The trees swoon with the rowdy wind, singing:
"Grasp it tight
Gasp for life
Gaps so bright
Gas the light to make new the night!"

Still...

My eyes are open to the sky. It is the only direction I can look for you. They grow heavy from the strain of the world. Make me water, the world oil. In but not of, together, but distinctly separate.

If I never speak again
If my hands shrivel.
If my legs wilt.
If my mouth splits in half.

If my son isn't
If my daughter never breaths
If I cannot see....

Be my sight. Let the tug of Your return pull me out of the darkness.

Wet Jeans

Ssssssweet and penetrating.
Wealthy and lush.
Delicate like an ornament and fragile like a baby.
Imprints of a finger and impressions of its tracks.
Sacred and secretive as whispers filtered through the heavens.
How I wish to begin to explain. How I have handled it so carelessly and rude?

I became so familiar... Too familiar I suppose. I tried to hold, but held with soaking hands.
No matter the angle, it will always fall without simply getting out of the sea and walking the dry land.
The waters so tempting; to get out after being in so long is uncomfortably cold. I would rather just sink in a bit and back up so it feels like space, the closest to space I'll ever know.
I can hear the crashing of the waves. I know how far I can go before they start to be a worry. It's still in my hands...I'm an excellent swimmer. The sand is furthering itself. We'll make it back. We always do, plus the water feels so nice.

Wait, what was I even first talking about? And why did I let us get out here so far? I held you first so dry and knew where I was going... Why did I think the water was okay? We don't even have our trunks on yet, and now my jeans are wet and it's harder to swim..

Rebirth

Flame Retardant

The flame flicks a prisoner of the wick. Such potential. For bulbs bring light, and heaters warmth, but neither can accomplish both like a flame. Its color shines innocence and its motion is persuasive, but its deceit is something marvelous. Consider what horror can come upon its release. It is nothing on its own; dependent upon others, yet devouring their aid. A shame to only exist at the expense of others. To wish to be set apart and move through the halls, searching for companionship as though its footsteps could bring purpose; there are only ashes. For whatever ignites is put to death and whatever keeps it suffers a martyrs death. Perhaps it is innocent? Does it even know? The hardwood floor of your house stand no chance to the connection of its touch. To not exist is impossible. To exist is detrimental. To live and move means its source of life must be punished. To live and move means it is completely and utterly dependent. How alike are we?

Ten Thousand Years

Life almost snuffed from the light: decisions decisions. The difference between life and never existing at all can come with an inflection of the heart or sensation of the will, large or small, brief or elongated. God gave the freedom, wisdom, discernment; you made the choice. How would you have known what would happen? Who knows, maybe I would make it? Maybe I'd take you? Maybe we would switch? Maybe nothing? Who, without a vision of the future, can number their own days or say "yes for sure" or "no, definitely." instead of: "I hope..."

Birthdays:Christmas:Easter: I love them all. I suppose if not, I wouldn't have noticed, maybe a brief spurt of pain, unbearable pain, but now at ten I don't remember being born, let alone the pain of birth. If it would have been a no, nothing missed, but since it was a yes, oh how much I love birthdays, friends, family, climbing trees, eating cake, running in the yard, enjoying the weather. Would you have missed me if you didn't even get to know me? Maybe? I could have been a number of things. Now I am. Maybe you would have liked me to be different and if I weren't I would have been the perfect child or a spoiled brat. Who would have told you different? The possibilities would have been endless: president? mayor? actor? Nothing bad of course, just potential heroes.

Are you rethinking your decision now? I shouldn't have been caught, it wasn't my plan. I had hoped to keep this from you but now that you know how I turned out, would it have been better for the world to have said no? It's not your fault, how could you have known? Maybe it was chance or maybe now I am an example for no. Nobody will know as long as you don't tell anyone, but if you say that you almost picked the alternative, who knows the storm of controversy. Maybe we say no in light of every evil in the world. If none are born, none can turn into what I have become. If all are silenced, none can be heroic either. But one thing we know is things look different in hindsight. Problems are solved and laughed at. But one thing I know is that it was a choice made. You made yours and I made mine. You would have ceased life from years. I stop a life with years. We could have had the same crime, would yours have been accepted because you are a parent and mine rejected because I was a stranger? How far down the depth of our choices can go. I live with yours and you live with mine.

We all can hold life in our hands. Oh how the Father loves life and the freedom of life. God, have mercy.

be

My feet planted on Your word seem dangerous and ridiculous. Such a small area.
How many ways can I be tossed to one side or the other? I've counted them and numbered them.
Then, how can it be that this is where You want me?

Yet, I trust in You. How many times have You saved me, even today?
Each star rests in the universe, placed by Your hand. You know their temperature and years.
Each planet, though easy to look at, marvel at, and learn has been crafted by You. You not only know it, You are why they are.

How can I speak? What can I say to You? I want Your presence, but there I am. How can I be with You without me? My eyes remind me of my failures. The feel of the air, hug of my shirt, the touch of my wedding ring; all good things, though they remind me that I am me, that I am nothing compared to You. I carry a heavy heart. No, maybe it's my mind. I don't even know how to speak. How to express myself. My words fall empty on the floor. Can you sift through it all to see what I mean?

Can I convince You to hear me? Do I have to bargain with You for love? How can I see You with tainted eyes, hear You with clogged ears? If I can't find you, are You there? Or am I even looking in the right place? You know the expanse of the sky, what makes up the sea, what thoughts and emotions truly are to

Your children. You have them better defined than we do; I wonder how You see them? What have we left in our discoveries that You have made more to discover? I want to know. I want to know You. In whatever way that is, I want to know You. How big is Your heart? How much do You care?

When there is death, that bridge You have crossed and defeated, when it comes to me, help me. I know You. Wherever it is You are, whether Heaven is anything like I imagine, whether the transition to You is cold or warm, whatever comes, let me know You. I want to not be surprised when I see Your face.

There You are. It's You. I know You.
That was You all that time?
I'm so filthy. How can I stand?

Ending

Part 3)
If my eyes could find you,
where would you be?
A soft, dedicated
human being,
with thick, blackened hair,
a wrinkling smile,
a braid on your cloak
that has been there a while.
Taken for birds,
mouths are opened and sour
Swinging from trees,
Toppling tower 'fter tower.
Holes in the hands of
your right and your left
hold the scissors to cut off
the slithers of death.
Vital to life and
singled in purpose
Bursting with fullness
while we still feel worthless.
Grate off our eyelids,
give us new eyes,
burn in the truth,
and eradicate lies.
 The End

Blood Hiccups

Blood.
Blood.
Blood.
Sickened, fainting. The sight makes my blood boil.
Cuts and scrapes become windows into the body and soul.
Biology, anatomy/ imagery, poetry.
Blood loss and blood let.
Human oil.
Squeamish: what have we but skin and hair?
Yes, until the arm is severed, stomach punctured; then we are so much more.
Give blood and get blood.
Categorically speaking, we are pretty close to the same.
O B positive (don't) B negative.
Costly
Priceless
Liquid gold, flowing through bodily straws.
Once flowed with water,
Flowing eternally
Giving eternally.
Red. Rich. Refreshed. Redeemed

Selfie

One day, please speak for me the words I could never find; more perfectly than I could ever imagine.
I feel the weight of sin in every word that comes out as I lose it and it gets received as it's heard, disconnected and withering with ever inching distance from my mouth.
But you say to me; speak. You say; give. You say to me; no, and yes.
I can be a frustrating mess. Does knowing that change it though?
I can only respond out of what I know, then after that it becomes permanent.
I'm creating history every day.
You don't change the past.
You only cover over it, taking the crumbles and piecing them into the future.
I'm the only one keeping record.

How am I supposed to be different from the world when it's all I've known?
   It feels unfair, uneasy, even unkind at times to make it so polarized.
You remind me. You speak truth. Before I was, I was in You. I'm more created to You.
   Biology isn't the most foundational, but my spirit.
As if words were created to fill the pages of books.

When my feet travel far, from the path to the field, still keep me close to your side.
When I can't find the sound of Your voice, I remember Your tone.

In the heavens my heart speaks louder than my mouth ever could,
and my cratered footprints reveal Your love for me.

The Hills Have Eyes

The mountains grow out of the earth, they shoot up from the ground; becoming the ground, like shifted clay squeezed in the hands of the Creator; nothing more is added, it just changes it's build and deepens the ocean, the only difference is the proximity to the heavens; the mountains reaching for the skies: the ground is everywhere, it only changes it's nearness to Heaven.

FI EL DS

Community shares the roles of beauty

It causes for purpose; known and potentialized
Growth is a process of...
* Early
* Middle
* End
Yet, for some, End is replaced with (continued)
Is there conflict? Is there not un-determined agreement?
Is there rebellion? If rebellion...there is independence
One alone is fine
2 together are good
Three can be indescribable
Yet, some without some make none
Some without some make just one still.
The light is light
The rain is rain
The seed is none without the 2
The soil is soil
The seed is none without the 1
The path is filled with split seeds
They plunged not, but dried
They sank not, but saw the tree
They were lured: they did not see
for growth, for beauty, for (continued)
They must bury, they must borrow, they must not split, but explode.
Community shares the role of beauty...
To die causes for community
To commune brings life.

The Sun, The Rain, The Soil, The seed
The Sun. The Rain. The Soil.

CUP

Son dial found rim chutes high in the summer heat. Bask a baby better than a man lost in age and manners. Disguise a planter in cloth and break to pieces the form of its bones to be a mess of structure. It takes longer to remember the truth of a moment than to rediscover it. But fury is bounced off of the walls of the skeleton of a home, without warning. Rip the paper out from the spine and wash it down until the trunk returns to brighter days, storied the same but the methods are twisted. When will never again. The seasons are never what they promise.

Backwash begins to taste like recycled mouth.
Filters cleanse only so much.
Purity comes when we spit.

Pimples

Night, salting the peppered ground, masking the sky and water in their reflections of each other. I dipped my toes underneath. Squished a spider crawling up from the water, ticking my leg. You caught me from across the pond and dove in, swimming over to talk, but my voice hurts from trying to get your attention. Moon light speckles the splashes from your head, in and out of the water, taking breaths. Feet dangle still, like a child in a chair too big. I heard they called an ambulance. That they didn't escape the fire. I heard his foot knocked the candle over during his sleep. Where were you when it was happening? I tried pushing the bottom of the house, trying to break it from the foundation and slide it into the pond. The bodies leaped from the windows, rolling in the pasture. When the ambulance arrived, they covered their flesh, put oxygen masks on, and drove off shrieking underneath the tree branches. You get to me, pushing yourself up onto the dock, your hand got splintered, so you pinch it out, but there's still a dark, ruby red, dripping down your palms. My face is red like your palms, until I saw your mark. It isn't the blood that surprised me. I ask you where it's from, but your voice is gone, worse than mine, a faint whisper spills into the water, making sounds of rain drops descending. Your hand points to the scene of the accident. I'm sorry. I didn't think you knew. My toes are freezing, and you should probably get something for that burn.

Nature's a Dictionary

Upper or lower, middle or not,
love makes the most of a blanket and rock
Underneath sky span, deep in the dirt,
life can be found in the stain on my shirt.
Weakening old knees, bloodied old hands,
death is a bird freed from cages on land
Slippery gripping, hastened the wind
holding me tight with the pains of my sin
Severing skin cells, bone cuts straight though
old crumbling body given to you.
Fear is disaster, hope a relief.
truth can be found on the imprint on leaves.
Failing to hold them, small peals of skin,
sealing my dried eyes, to see you again.
SkyRiverAspen, MountainousPeak
Words don't bring meaning, unless He should speak.

You are the true one, You I adore,
You're bringing peace in the midst of this war.

Raven Wings/Wedding Feast

      he woke up this morning with an itching in his back. the bed was covered in black and grey feathers. it hasn't been easy sitting and typing at his job, but he had made it through, day after day. they make fun of the cape made of oily, torrid barbules and barb. it gets heavy and the calamus scratches him, as if the quill was printing ink upon his back, writing his death warrant. jerry, the accounting guy, called him birdman and tripped him in the hall. fly, birdman. they turn the heat up, sweat doesn't drip far, but builds up and collects at the bottom, trickling off the tips. after work, he headed to his car; his legs were sticky with honey, his hair matted with syrup. the path was full of thorns and thistles, his socks became wet as he didn't see a pot hole, filled with water, yet stepped into it and fell, mangling his knees. if he still had a heart, the scrapes and bruises and wounds made it nearly impossible to find inside his chest: maybe it had fallen or drained down to his ankles. after the darkness hovered where the light once reigned, he pulled into his parking spot. his brief case broke open as he pulled it from the back seat, battling against the seat belt. walking the steps, he wiped the tears from his fur-covered cheeks.

Oh, Sweet resting place, blessed dwelling; A Sanctum.
He dropped the cape, pealed the stiff stockings from his feet, and showered, washing the grime and stench of the day away, down the drain into the sewer.
It was brighter in the room than it had been all day.

He washed his face, his feet, in between his fingers and toes, oh are you serious!

Kiwis!
Strawberries!
Purified water!
He had put a pair of socks in his dryer when he got home, and put them on once he was finished showering.
Clean shirts!
Fresh Sheets!
His apartment looked out over at the mountains and, lemonade in hand, he saw a radiance near the foothills. The best way to describe the sight:

There were seventeen arena-sized parachutes, suspended in the sky, pouring effulgence from underneath upon the grassy hills and calm meadows. Lingering, like colossal jelly fish mangled in the air, yet comfortable. End of times for many, maybe, but the light, to him, was like an awareness or safety of parents in the next room, the light coming in through the crack in the door.

He climbed into his clean bed, the sheets smelled like fabric softener and his pillow was cool on both sides. His mental theater and dreams glided into each other and he rested...until the morning.

(Oh God, so are You to me.)

time is given to you.
don't let it slip away.

How easily a tear drop can turn the whole thing to mud.
Stuck in between your toes, tracked in onto the carpet.

Wipe them away.

Glasses

Where can a man find rest? In the pockets of his mind or in the space of the wild? In God's hearts lays droves of resting souls. Resting, in a place not seen with human eyes or heard with ears, not found with the mind or discovered merely by chance. Can there be rest in a world with others? We are people unable to control the minds and hearts of others, but only the tinglings in our own spirit, through our own souls; yet we are called to love, to care for, to be the other's keeper. If I can't control myself, how can I rest when I can't control you? Age brings wisdom brings sorrow brings a disconnect from itself. The world hasn't made memory of the countless footprints on its skin; it doesn't see a special face and give it the secret to eternity. Eternity lives in the hearts of men. My mind wouldn't recognize my younger body, nor would I be suited now for the future. I think I don't change, but I am a different man each day. A late night look through the window sees the passing of another day:

Tomorrow will come, even if not for me. Tomorrow will come and be as present as the past, near as the future. If I see the stars, it'd be too late. A constant that was born from a constant, unborn, immovable. God hasn't been so far removed by men at all; He moves in our midst, in front of our face, within our hearts. He breathes life in the next room, watches for a movement of the spirit, stirs the depths of our understand. He is not far from anyone. Eternity sweats with His love.

At The End Of The Day •

Remember
Ember of membery
Memory. Right. But
Every flight.
Fighting a system of right
Of wrong. Of bad.
Of mad and sad.
A sad is a picture
But picture I had.
Forgotten it all.
It swells like a fall
A swelling. A ball. A
damage of skin to
Remember the fall.
Forgetten.
Forgotten is right.
A light in the dark
To brighten with sight
A light that is seen
A love and a day
That remain as a dream
But I want when I wake
To think of your face
And to locate the trace
That unravelled back to you.
It's not right.
Unfair that my light
Only shines.
At night. Last night
When I held you so close
Held it tight.

I don't want to think
But to live it still.
Membery fades
Memory. Right. But
Clears away at the end of.
The day, and tomorrow
Will too fade away.
All the same.
But now.
With my name.
We can create tomorrow
A membery same
To hold close.
So we never remain
In the previous days.
But each one can still
A new day exclaim.

Supplication

Oh, turn back towards the light and see the furrowed ground behind, for when you run with hopes to spite the dirt and grass in hand He'll bind.

He blanketed the earth in love, the seas and sky were bound in blue, deepest colors, richest sounds, best sensations, gifts to you!

At once a tender, ragged wound, sensitive and bloody brown
from gripping earth and shaking to, to bring you back on solid ground.

Facelessly

Yellow my heart, Yellow my eyes, Y
ellow your powdered silhouette. Ye
llow you spoke out, Yel
low the Sun. Yellow the birds dressed in Yell
ow twine. Yellow the flowers first sprinkled in blue.
w the bushfire burning for you. Yellow my anger,
ow my pride. Yellow insides Yellow up wide. Yel
low breasted Chats, Yellow garden tools, Ye
llow wind inside my ears. Yellow my lungs. Y
ellow the cheeks of a Yellow born baby.
Yellow screams for truth. Yellows blood red.
Yellows no place for lies to make their bed.
 Yellows the loose knitted sweater for him
  Yellows the shirt from the cotton gin.
 Yellow the bountiful blessings within
Yellow the plentiful messings of sin.
ellow my heart when it's given away
llow the switchblade, Yellow the tears
low the opening in the clouds. Yellow the Heavens
ow a wounded man on the ground.
w the vanishing visceral sound.
the treasure of freeing the bound.

Forfeit

On record, the sound's the same.
History preserved through modern techniques calculate the future.
A pile of broken dishwashers and heavy disdain.

On record, the people seem tame.
Blissfully deserving the war churned defeat of a country sutured.
A while ago, nobodies suffered and died without fame.

On the surface, I am a rickety house, old and cracked by the winds of change.
Inside, on the dresser, my heart rests, exposed and freezing.
Blow through the house, rustle the windows with the sound of your name.
Your gusts, though strong, will hold me tight.

Brittle STRucturrrre e s...

Back sliden
Black, ridden soul.
Hidden mold.
Cold quickened,
Bitten poll.
Lack spitten: bold.
Track lipping.

Waking proud
Making loud sounds
Shrouds found
Ground cloud
plowed down
Shaking crowd pounds
Aching rounds.

Scolding fire
Holding wired shapes
Tired tapes
Gate buyers
Hired apes
Molding mire plates
Folding liars

Hollow praise
Swallowed graves dug
Waves shrugged
Mugged ways
Shave love
Shallowed haze bug
Borrowed days

Recycling

I will walk till my legs become thick, wooden trunks,
roots sunken far below the soil, gripping the underneath,
making it to the surface of another life;
flowers blooming up from the earth, pleasing to Your sight...

Botched Carpentry

Spit stuck terrace burning ether bright.
Gated brick backdrop painted pale white.
Heaven on par with infants at night.
Fight, little dandled ones. Fight for your life.

I draw water from deepening land.
Smoothed out dimples, brushed soft from your hand.
Fill the details with curative sand.
Stand with broken backs, as long as you can.

Blood siphoned thick through telephone wire.
Puncture cells charred brown soot in the fire.
Heart stopped cold off the end of a spire.
Higher suns don't know they flare any higher.

Grace sparks response out of hopes and fears.
Love moves inside without aid from ears.
Truth seeps down despite calendar years.
Tears singe their pathway when He's drawing near.

powerless saviours

I) Basked in nast' sin, dye it blonde. Skin and bones and heart to hide.
Gas and Aspirin, final song, stay up late and wait to die.

II) Tasks (congrats!) have got it wrong, nothing ever satisfies.
The cast of 'Cats' been going strong, but no, not one of them survives.

III) Blast that vast brim, grip the tong, grab the neck and wring it dry
How fast the fastened triggers song has stolen broken heart's goodbyes.

IV) Axe the past, man, it's all gone. Forgive them, no need to cry.
Grasp an aspen, ride it long. Swing it back and let it fly.

V) At last, relax and join along with angels singing out on high
while the entire time you were trying to make something on your own, His love was being poured out over you.

This is serious.

(Five 2 lined poems all relating to one another, in one way or another.)

Eight of Them, Already.

Rue. Heart pressed for a swiftness of
ocean air, a whisper from the gulf.
Unraveled in a wool caption. Don't go.
Stay. Release. Revive. Bright without light. Awake
without sight. My feet haven't been bare
for years, too busy to take them
out. I want to Adam the ground.
To see a moment stay. I want
the fall to not be *already* or
only, but autumn. Impossible to count the
passing gusts, or even categorize. They move
on another scale. They move despite any
intention of the heart. How can the
length of time be measured when our
mind is more vast, more profound than
we know? There are caverns inside my
mind collecting webs, spiders inhabit when I
have yet to understand how to reach
them. I want to be more. I
want to experience more than the senses
can tolerate. Internally combustive by a truth
about life that is at my grasp.
The pale, teal leaves of my toes
peel back and reveal an even paler
paled green of shedding skin. If I'm
a tree, you are the seed to
sprout my growth. Making bark sears as
it cracks to its solid. Years of
life trace by the spirals in my
spirit. Don't die. Come home. Let's reach
for the clouds in a whim of

jealousy. They stand so much closer to
Heaven. The seasons of my eyes and
heart are as cold as winter, but
come summer, I will see the world
through the warmth of love. With dirt
on my toes and sand in my stomach.

.Smokeless Campfire.

Faking a signal to form a rebellion,
touch can still settle the heart of a hellion but none
more so than You.
Pages are turned, white paper is beaming
It's smoky inside the mind of a free man
the blur disguises the fact that it's freezing but there's
nothing more one can do.
Anxious followers following writers
writing the words of passed away fighters
fighting for something to make them feel lighter
but lighters are those who had started the fires but
nobody thinks that it's true.
Admission ignites perspicacious vocality
signaling spacious insights to morality
blends thin particulars into totality
spotting the covered, concealed specialty
breaching the tight eyes to see true reality but still
only but a glimpse of You
Sprained wrist twisting to swivel a rocking chair-
Balding scalp scratched with the motion of brushing
hair-
Tree trunk refastens to tree with the utmost care-
Cancerous heartache snuffed out without any wear-
Smoke retracing its tracks to the burning flare-
Filthy and clouded out eyes without any glare but still
nothing better than You.

Birthing classes

I haven't forgotten you. You've never forgotten me. Through these years, you never left. You don't grow bored or tired like I do. At this point, I never thought til here. Decades of expectations. Gone by with the blink of an eye. I can't imagine what's next, but I'll be there before I know it. Looking back on this time, wondering what I've done. I'm being whittled down to a few strong hobbies and interests that I can hold on to, possibilities disappear into a mist of old ideas, unrealized and locked in a cage of my younger mind. Could I have done anything I set my mind to? What could I be doing now that I'll think back on and see the urgency of the time.
I love a few things now while loving everything. I love a few people now while loving everyone. Like taught ropes of connection, snapping under the pressure and leaving me untethered. Maybe it's the difference between love and acquaintance. Love and tolerance. Love and.
But life's a beam of light, funneled down to the floor, speckles of dust passing in and out of sight, some floating for longer, before the sun sets and the light moves on, to light some other room. You are the light. You are the window. The room. You can't leave, there'd be no light without You, and then. There'd be no me. Decrease my opacity so Your light can shoot through me.

Lady MacBeth

My father puts on his orange hat and flannel vest and I mimic his wardrobe. The house is warm to battle the cold that creeps in from the changing of the seasons. I climb the chair to see the pond as my dad tells me it's going to freeze over soon. Peering out I see the gray, blue sky and brown grass border the fog in between as the forest, separating our house from the rest of the world, becomes dim. My dad helps me get my boots on, tying them tight and pulling my jeans over the laces. He zips up his coat as he grabs his shotgun by the barrel and slides open the door, without saying a word. He has attempted to take me with him for what seems like years now, but I have never agreed. I have outgrown the outfits but he continued to get the same clothes in different sizes up until now. I suppose I'm ready. I hop the steps and follow behind him.

As we walk away from the house I turn back to see the chimney blow smoke from its top and already miss the warmth. It doesn't take long for my pants to hike up over my boots as they collect water, drenching my socks inside. The weeds are high and we break branches with our steps to the perfect spot. I never know what it is he hunts for, but my guess would be pheasant since the only other wildlife near the house are frogs, toads, ribbon snakes, and the occasional beaver. Suddenly, a flock of common quail break from a group of giant cane rush and fly into the air in a flutter of feathers and grass, yet my father remains calm and continues walking a few more steps. As I follow him he stops me, turns and gets down on a knee. He looks me in the eye and motions for me to back step a few feet, lifting his gloved fingers when I'd gone far enough. I see my dad load his weapon and reconnect the neck of his gun. He points it at me, but I am not afraid of him; he's my dad.

    A few moments later I see another grouping of birds rise from the ground as my stomach feels a sharp pain like I have never felt. It warms my body and blacks out my eyes. My shirt feels wet and cold as I feel my dad putting pressure on my chest with his gloves. With my eyes barely opened I see him handling body parts; a heart, lung, liver, and spleen. It looks like he is putting them in my jacket, but instead he places them back inside of me. The gray of the sky gets darker as he picks me up with one hand to carry me back to the house, gripping his weapon in the other. My head resting on his shoulder, I look back and see the long black needle rush drenched with blood and bits of my coat. That night, I try to remember if it was a dream or if it was real. Either way, I am not scared of my father, but instead maybe know him better. Wrapped in a blanket, sitting on a wooded stool in the dining room, I see him wash and remove his gloves, placing them on a dishtowel on the counter. His gloves are now clean; yet I wonder, why is there still blood on his hands?

the darkest alley

Docile downey, downing and gaunt
A fable, a feeble attempting a want
A waking, a shaking, a flower of gold
A smell of a smattering, gauntlet of old •

The darker the alley the sharper the cut
A shooting sensation right into the gut
A secular outing made sacred in time
With streetlights highlighting a skeleton brine •

A cross and a cradle, a cover of red
A bottle that settles the scent of the dead
To battle the wicked and will of the heart
To startle the treacherous right from the start •

To die is to diddle a doorknob or two
To wish it, to want it to unstick the glue
Both swiftly and softly uncouthly begin
To riddle the suction of perilous sin •

Understandable for some, but not for me. I don't understand it. I want to though...
(The Title)

God, how can you stand it?
Stand evil
Stand the world
Stand me?

How can you stand it? The sand pit, the trenches, expanded and taken by satanic bandits.
How can you stand all the pain and the torture handed over by evil's plans? It becomes a brutally heartbreaking task to see the enemy work so hard in areas where the light seems dim. I know you have victory over the enemy, but how long till he's gone?

How can you bear it? I sweat it can take but a tear into truth to rid earth of it's merit.
How can you bear when your people take scripture and turn it to make what's crooked seem straight? I see the dust on our Bibles till someone reliable says something uncomfortable and we look for verses of cheap grace or love as equal to complete tolerance of anything.

How do you love me? Above me, you see that to hug me produces my kicking and shoving.
How do you love when I rebel for no reason? I battle myself to see clearly, the way I want to, the way I need to, yet I resist. Don't you tire of me? Do I wear you down? I make you react to me so differently than

I know you do, yet knowing isn't seeing as I crave it to be yet.

I am worn by it all. You've been since. You have seen every detail of our miserable lives. You don't stand, you love.
Thank you. Oh God, thank you...

Bastion

Bummed out. Hands dripping with a cold sweat. The doors open and close, but the color has driven away out since yesterday. Fluorescent light clearing you out, like I sanitize to be sterile and blanched. Don't take the orange, like a setting sun. I can't follow it, instead the waves stretch and iron out to a blank fitted sheet. I could see it before. I swear. The heat from the cement drives baking my cheek and I flip sides, like a hot/cool side of a pillow. Fuzzy like a peach, spit shined in my own reflection each morning, without years of recognition, but months. Not, just. Back that far before I hadn't been, but now, I remember a lifetime. Days scratch with trimmed nails, the Septembers, down to it's weather, down to it's date, down to a Monday, down to a 7 O'Clock, down. Floor looks back to the sky. But yet, not. Set. Wake. Wait. Wa. Walk down the corner. To the bastion
in a broken tooth. Seared air. Ivory both cracked and sent in manila. Oh, God. Linger. Don't cap. Don't heal. Gape. Crack the sky. Break the earth. Bleed the ocean until it's hue explodes to executing blue. Break my glasses to reveal the jest in a pirate patch for sight, when there's nothing to hide apart from my own separating oakum and a god my mind has made to replace who You are. So at wained. Sutcher me with Your Gold and Combination Whiteeeeeeeeeeeeeeeeeeeeeeeeeeeee

Resplendent Birth

(Your) Words create, held in stiffened hands, tossed into the air, made into earth. I could only hear them.

(and) Light

here

    like water

        over the whole of the universe. ethereal.
                unbelievably... true.

    near all beings.

inside

outside.

I want to see You outside.
I promise I won't talk.
Let's go outside.

Hiraeth

Bathed in the bright summer swimming below
Shiver in caverns by dim mellow glow
Biting the coin to see if it's real gold
Uncertain as to which way is down.
But certain the warmth of the ground

Falling asleep in the back of the car
Sopping head resting on top of my arm
Sun drips behind smoke signals of cigars
Concrete this moment in memory
Wash away this foul century

All that I need is a kiss on the mouth
A squeeze of my hand and a trip to the south
A corner bar, sitting away from the crowds
Just sitting, just watching you move me
Sway with changes in scenery

Circling toes into patterns of dirt
Wiping my eyes in the crease of my shirt
Laughing with you as we're shedding the hurt
Examine my eyes for the traces
Dry off the tears from our faces

Petrichor feeling too much like a home
Memory fighting to make it your own
Praying and knowing your never alone
Home is still not a place you reside
But residence inside His light

A Frame

There are places I feel at home that may never be created, dreams of homes that cannot exist, but I feel them in my heart, like a memory of who I am, who I was born to be and where

Not made of wood, or stone or brick.
Not a home with the morning light beaming through the cracks in the drapes.
Not a home of lavender and pine, tobacco and cinder.
Not a home of creaking bamboo flooring or chalky brisk pavement.
Not a home in the forest, by the beach, or down the pavement at the corner

If there is a home to be shared it's made of else.

Three stories, but the floors won't hold. The cracks have taken over the substance, as it sways with the wind.

.

I climb to the top, looking for the voice coming through the walls, until you reach for me through the scene and pull me out to your reality. Lose my sight and sound, until I find your home as a place I would not have been able to describe without you.

Townie

Immersed into a dirt constructed paradigm, he has found the impression of a child, left in the background. Depending on the time of year, whether the third day or not, the sphere of life shifts; making light the dark, and heights the deep. Space compressed in a vacuum, instantly changing the future's past into a grain of sand, too heavy to hold but available to all who grasp. The safe route back becomes the one with the most dangerous outcome, unknown to the traveler: perhaps dismissed? For once a rock is taken out of place to toss into the water, the bugs scatter; they have already lost their security, it is dismantled. Yet, he saw the rocks, the insects, the ripples in the water, he did not dismay, for in the process of faith and the sequence of a journey, he chose to take the blame of all who tilted the foundations and with such precise implementation, altered the chaos into beauty.

The water still ripples, but only for a time.

One day, all will be made new

Made in the USA
Coppell, TX
29 December 2023